Hedgehog Of Moon Meadow Farm

Lynne Garner

Hedgehog of Moon Meadow Farm
Copyright © Lynne Garner 2018
Published by Mad Moment Media
www.madmomentmedia.com

Lynne Garner has asserted her right under the Copyright, Designs
and Patent Act 1988 to be identified as the author of this work.

ISBN 978-1-9996807-2-5

Mad Moment Media is a trading name of Nyrex Limited
Flourish on front cover by Nenikime – freepik.com
Cover illustration and design by Debbie Knight

DEDICATION

Thank you, Trudi, for 'that' conversation and thank you, Jon, for your unwavering support of my love for my prickly friends. Finally thank you, Helen, friend and vet extraordinaire.

CONTENTS

INTRODUCTION

I never intended to write another collection of short stories (this is my fourth), it just sort of happened. Many years ago, a close friend, Trudi, and I were enjoying a light-hearted conversation about hedgehogs and the various and often strange uses they have been put to down the centuries. During that conversation, an idea for a hedgehog-based non-fiction book began to germinate. Every so often this work in progress has been resurrected and a little more research carried out. On my last attempt to get this non-fiction title to first draft, I realised I had enough material for a new story collection. So I got to work writing a retelling of the traditional stories I'd collected and the result is this book.

The ten stories that follow originate in many different parts of the world. However, I decided to set my stories in the English countryside. So our hedgehog enjoys wandering the lanes and woods of the countryside and the fields of a small family-run farm called Moon Meadow Farm. Our Hedgehog supports his friends when he can, but when given the chance he will also use his wits to show them just how clever a hedgehog can be.

I hope you enjoy the stories as much as I've enjoyed researching and writing them.

Lynne Garner, May 2017

Please note: To keep the authentic feel of the English countryside we've kept to English (UK) spelling and terms throughout this book.

"Here's a good rule of thumb: too clever is dumb."

Ogden Nash (1902 – 1971)

HEDGEHOG'S THREE WITS

It was early spring, a time of year Hedgehog loved. It meant the autumn leaves were still covering the ground and he'd find something nice to eat hidden under them. As he rummaged there was a wonderful rustling, quickly followed by a sound of contented munching whilst he feasted on centipedes, millipedes and bugs of all sorts.

As Hedgehog foraged in the dim light of the setting sun he didn't notice Fox sitting, half hidden, in a bush on the side of the meadow.

"Evening," said Fox as Hedgehog got near to where he was sitting.

Hedgehog jumped and quickly pulled himself into a tight ball, his spines now an impenetrable shield.

Fox laughed, then said, "Hedgehog, it's only me. No need to worry."

Hedgehog uncurled and sniffed the air. Recognising the scent of his friend, he quickly uncurled some more and smiled.

"What are you up to?" asked Hedgehog, knowing his friend wouldn't simply be sitting quietly taking in the cool evening air. Fox was always up to something.

"Planning," replied Fox, with a sly smile.

"Planning what?" asked Hedgehog.

Fox nodded towards the old chicken coop on the other side of the meadow. "I've been watching the humans rebuild the chicken coop," he said. "They've made it to keep the chickens in, but not to keep me out. They've forgotten how crafty I can be."

Hedgehog looked at the coop and licked his lips. "I've seen what they throw down for the chickens and some of it looks very tasty," he said. "I wouldn't mind getting in there myself."

Fox chuckled. "Out of a hundred, how many wits would you give yourself, my dear friend?"

"On a scale of one hundred, I'd give myself three," replied Hedgehog. "I know what I need to know and nothing more."

"Then you'll need my help," replied Fox. "On a scale of one hundred, I'd give myself at least seventy-seven, if not higher."

"Then it's my lucky night," replied Hedgehog.

"Yes, it is," said Fox.

Just then the farm door opened and the light pushed back the darkness which covered the meadow. The air was suddenly filled with the excited barking of the sheepdog as she came bounding out of the door and across the meadow.

"I'll see you here tomorrow evening," said Fox. "I'll get us into that coop." He then slipped into the leaves of the bush and was soon out of sight.

Hedgehog looked across the meadow to see the sheepdog running towards him, her tongue and ears flapping. Knowing he'd never outrun her, Hedgehog pulled his head under and got ready. Feeling her warm breath on his back, Hedgehog hissed and, using his front legs, he jerked his head up. The sheepdog yelped as Hedgehog's spines pierced her tender nose. Hedgehog hissed and jerked his head a second time. The sheepdog yelped again, turned around and ran back to the safety of the farmhouse.

Hedgehog waited for a while, then slowly uncurled and returned to rummaging and rustling among the leaves.

•

The next evening Hedgehog returned to the same spot and as he waited for Fox he rummaged among the leaves for a tasty morsel or two. Hedgehog had just found a long, succulent centipede when Fox's face peered out of the bush.

"Evening," said Fox, making Hedgehog jump.

"I wish you wouldn't do that," said Hedgehog, almost choking on the centipede he'd not quite swallowed.

Fox chuckled and asked, "Are you ready to break into that chicken coop?"

Hedgehog thought about all those lovely things the farmer's wife threw down for the chickens and licked his lips. "I am," he said. "Have you worked out how to break into the coop?"

"I have an idea or two," replied Fox. "We did agree I had more wits than you do."

"Yes, you did, didn't you?" said Hedgehog.

"Then let's go," said Fox. "I'm hungry."

As the friends crept across the meadow they chatted about this and that, that and this.

"We'd better keep an eye out for that sheepdog," said Hedgehog. "I managed to fend her off last night, but I'm not sure my one trick will work again."

"There's – nooooooo …" howled Fox, as he disappeared into a large, deep hole.

"Fox, what …?" said Hedgehog as he tumbled head over tail into the hole. Landing with a bump, Hedgehog thought, Thank goodness for my spines.

"Hedgehog, Hedgehog are you there?" whimpered Fox.

Hedgehog quickly uncurled. "Yes, just a little dazed," he replied. "Are you all right?"

"I think so," Fox replied. "Where did this hole come from? It wasn't here last night."

"I'm not worried about that. I'm worried about how we're going to get out," said Hedgehog.

"Don't worry, I'm sure to come up with an idea," said Fox confidently.

Fox fell silent for a while and paced around and around the hole looking for an escape route.

"It's too narrow for me to run and jump," said Fox. "And the sides are too steep for me to climb."

"How are we going to get out?" asked Hedgehog. "I thought you had more wits than I have."

"I do," snapped Fox, frustrated he couldn't come up with an idea.

Hedgehog began to pace up and down. "Oh, I'm

beginning to feel unwell," he said. "It must be that fall."

"I'll come up with something," said Fox. "Just give me a little time."

"I'm beginning to feel very unwell," said Hedgehog. "I think I'm going to be …"

"Don't you dare!" said Fox.

"I'm sorry," said Hedgehog, who was very unwell in the corner of the hole.

"That's all we need," said Fox.

"I'm sorry," said Hedgehog. "I think I'm going to …"

"No, you don't!" Fox shouted, as he scooped Hedgehog up into his paws and threw him into the air and over the edge of the hole.

Hedgehog landed with a gentle thump on the soft meadow grass. He uncurled and smiled to himself. He looked over the edge of the hole and said, "Fox, you are clever. Thank you."

"How am I going to get out?" asked Fox, frustrated.

"Why ask me?" asked Hedgehog. "I only have three wits, remember? You have seventy-seven."

Fox sat at the bottom of the hole and shook his head. "I'm done for," he said.

"I'm sorry," said Hedgehog. "I wish I could help."

Hedgehog went to leave, stopped and slowly turned around. "Fox," he said, as he peered over the edge of the hole. "Although I only have three wits, I have an idea."

"I'll try anything," Fox replied.

"Lie very still next to where I was unwell," said Hedgehog. "Keep your eyes open and stick your tongue out."

"Why would I do that?" asked Fox.

"When the farmer comes, he'll think you're dead and will throw you on the compost heap," Hedgehog told Fox. "When he's not looking, you can creep away."

Fox smiled. "You may only have three wits, Hedgehog, but it's a good three."

Just then the farmhouse door opened and the barking of the sheepdog could be heard.

"I'll see you soon, my friend," said Hedgehog, who scurried across the meadow and disappeared into the hawthorn hedge.

• • •

HEDGEHOG'S THREE WITS

*"It is not safe to join interests with strangers upon such terms
as to lay ourselves at their mercy."*

Samuel Richardson (1689 – 1761)

HEDGEHOG AND SNAKE

As the seasons changed the leaves began to turn from their many shades of green to the golden yellows and oranges of autumn. The nights became colder, the first light frost had painted the grass white and Hedgehog had begun to think about winter.

It's time for me to start building my winter nest, he thought. I'd better start looking for just the right place.

So, between snacking on worms, slugs and snails, he looked for a safe place to build his winter nest. He looked around the edges of the flower meadow, in the small woods at the bottom of the valley and in the farmer's garden. As the first few rays of the morning sun began to come over the horizon, Hedgehog found just what he was looking for: a sheltered nesting place hidden between the tatty wooden fence and the tumbled-down shed.

"This should do," he said to himself. He yawned, rubbed his eyes and added, "I need some sleep. I'll start work tomorrow."

•

As soon as the sun was replaced by the moon, Hedgehog

poked his small black nose out of his nest and smelt for danger. No one was around and all was quiet.

He crept out from his warm nest and shivered. "No time to lose. Winter with her thick frosts and snow will soon be here."

That night Hedgehog searched for dry leaves and grasses to line his new nest. He gathered leaves from under the oak tree at the edge of the woods, grasses from the flower meadow and even a few large, strange-looking leaves from the farmer's garden. Between gathering the leaves and grasses, Hedgehog stopped to snack on the odd slug, snail and spider. Finally, as he wove the last leaf into place, he sighed and said, "That's a relief. I'd hate to be sleeping in my old nest when winter hits."

For the first few nights all was well and Hedgehog's new winter nest was warm and comfortable. However, that changed when the first winter storm ripped the trees from their roots and the stream broke its banks. As the other animals took shelter, Hedgehog watched the howling wind demolish the tumbled-down shed and take his nest away a leaf and blade of grass at a time.

By the time the storm had passed Hedgehog was soaked through to the skin, cold and homeless. Miserable, he returned to his old nest, which had managed to survive the storm, but was wet and cold. He climbed into it, tried to get comfortable and dozed the day away.

•

As it was getting dark Hedgehog crept out of his nest and shook the damp leaves off his spines. Cold and unhappy, he sighed and muttered to himself, "I suppose I'd better find another nesting place."

So he skirted around the edges of the flower meadow, looked among the roots of the gnarled oak trees in the woods, and checked the farmer's garden again.

"I'm never going to find a good spot at this rate," he said, shaking his head. Just then the clouds parted. The full moon shone down and covered the land in a pale yellow light. Hedgehog noticed part of the dry stone wall by the gate had collapsed. "Perhaps there would be a good place."

Hedgehog wandered over to the dry stone wall and looked between the large stones. "This will do nicely," he said to himself.

Then Hedgehog heard a voice. "This'll be just right."

Hedgehog froze for a moment and quietly asked, "Who's that?"

Everything was silent; not even the wind moved.

Slowly a small greenish head poked around the corner of a large rock. Hedgehog breathed a sigh of relief when he recognised the yellow and black markings and the small round black and yellow eyes.

"Hello, Snake," he said. "What are you up to?"

"I'm looking for a place to hibernate," she replied. "My normal place is full of my family and friends. It's far too crowded, so I was looking for a new place and I think I've found it here."

"I lost my winter nest last night," Hedgehog told Snake. "Perhaps we could share."

Snake looked in the hole in the rocks, thought for a

while, then said, "It'll be a bit of a squeeze."

"Give me a little time to find some leaves and grasses and it'll be just right," said Hedgehog.

"All right then," Snake said, reluctantly.

By the time Hedgehog returned with his first mouthful of leaves Snake had slipped into the hole and made herself comfortable on a small pile of soil at the back of the hole. For the rest of the night Hedgehog ran to and fro filling the hole with leaves and grass. As the weak winter sun rose above the woods he returned with the last mouthful of leaves.

"There you go," he said. "Just in time."

As Hedgehog turned around to flatten the bottom of his nest he trod on Snake's tail.

"Ouch!" said Snake.

"Sorry," said Hedgehog. "I'm not used to sharing."

He quickly settled down and was soon gently snoring. As he slept, Hedgehog dreamt of catching earwigs, beetles and slugs and as he dreamt, he wiggled.

"Ouch!" said Snake, trying to move out of Hedgehog's way.

Hedgehog continued to snore and dream.

"Ouch!' said Snake, as Hedgehog's spines pierced her skin again.

Finally, Snake had had enough.

"Hedgehog, wake up!" she said, angry. But Hedgehog continued to snore. "HEDGEHOG!"

"What, what?" asked Hedgehog, slowly opening his eyes.

"You keep spiking me with your spines," said Snake.

"We can't share. You'll have to find somewhere else to go."

"Why should I go?" asked Hedgehog.

"I found this nesting place first," said Snake.

"No, you didn't," replied Hedgehog, now fully awake.

"Yes, I did," hissed Snake.

"Even if you did," said Hedgehog, "I filled it with warm leaves and grass. So you should go."

"I didn't ask you to make a nest," said Snake.

"I'm not budging," said Hedgehog, firmly. "You have somewhere to go. I don't." Hedgehog turned his back on Snake, snuggled down and went back to sleep.

Snake, realising she'd lost, shook her head, slithered out of the hole and made her way to join her family and friends.

• • •

"The fox knows many tricks, and the hedgehog only one;
but that is the best one of all."

Archilochus (680BC – 645BC)

HEDGEHOG, FOX AND THE FLIES

It was that time of year when it wasn't quite winter, but it wasn't quite spring. The time of year when one night it's warm with a full, bright moon and the next there's a howling wind and stinging rain. Sadly, for Hedgehog and his friends, this night was one of those nights. The rain was falling in torrents and the sky was full of flashing lights and rumbling thunder.

"I'm not going out in this," said Hedgehog as he looked outside.

Hedgehog breathed a sigh of relief when eventually the storm moved on. "I can't put it off any longer," he told himself as his stomach gave a low, long grumble. He stepped on to the wet grass and was soon enjoying his fill of slugs, snails and woodlice.

It was almost daybreak and Hedgehog started to head home. "I'll take the short cut down by the stream," he said to himself. As he neared the stream, Hedgehog found himself wading knee-deep through cold water. The stream had burst its banks and taken up a new, temporary home in the cows' field.

As he splashed through the water, Hedgehog heard a familiar voice groaning. He followed the voice and found his friend, Fox, draped over a tree trunk, bruised and battered.

"Fox," said Hedgehog, as he waded through the water. "What happened?"

"When the storm came I slipped into the stream and it washed me down to here," replied Fox weakly.

"Let me help you," said Hedgehog, as he put out a paw.

Fox winced and groaned as his friend helped him off the tree trunk.

"Will you be all right?" asked Hedgehog.

"It's just cuts and bruises," said Fox. "But I'm very tired. Can you help me to that bush?"

"You need to get home to your den," said Hedgehog, trying to ignore the sun as it began to appear over the horizon.

"You need to get back to your nest and I need to rest," said Fox, wincing. "I can sleep here."

"Are you sure?" asked Hedgehog.

"I'm sure," said Fox. "I can hide myself away. The farmer won't let the cows graze in this field today."

Hedgehog helped his friend to the bush and watched as he hid among its low-hanging branches.

"I can stay," said Hedgehog.

"No, go," Fox said. "I'll be fine here."

So, although he didn't want to leave his friend, Hedgehog reluctantly returned to his nest.

•

As Hedgehog snuggled down in his nest all he could think about was his friend lying under the bush.

"I'll check on him tomorrow," Hedgehog told himself as he closed his eyes. But every time he dropped off to sleep Hedgehog was woken by bad dreams about his friend. He dreamt the sheepdog found him and dragged him out from under the bush. He dreamt the farmer discovered him and took him away. He dreamt the cows were allowed into the field and trampled the bush.

"I give up," said Hedgehog. "I just have to check on Fox." So even though the sun hadn't fully set, Hedgehog snuck out of his nest and, keeping to the shadows, made his way to the bush. When he got there all he could hear was a low continuous buzz.

"Fox, Fox," called Hedgehog. "Are you there?"

"Yes," replied Fox softly.

Hedgehog crawled into the bush and found Fox covered in flies. "My dear friend, they're eating you alive. I'll get rid of them for you."

"No, please don't," replied Fox, as his long tail and ears twitched involuntarily.

"I must do something."

"Please leave them."

"How can I?" asked Hedgehog. "There are so many of them and they're eating you alive."

"They've pestered me all day and are full up," said Fox. "If you scare them away they'll only be replaced by hungry friends who will drain me dry."

"You're right," said Hedgehog. "You do have more wits

than me."

Hedgehog smiled and sat with his friend until the sun set and the flies left to sleep off their full stomachs.

• • •

"The whole hedgehog is prickly."

Desiderius Erasmus Roterodamus (1466 – 1536)

HEDEGHOG VERSES HARE

Hedgehog skirted around a bush and pounced on a large bright green caterpillar. "Delicious," he said, swallowing it whole.

Suddenly Hare rushed passed and knocked Hedgehog over. "Be careful," shouted Hedgehog. "I was eating."

Hare turned on his heels and ran back to Hedgehog. "Don't live in the slow lane and get in my way then," he said.

"Slow lane, indeed," said Hedgehog, his prickles rising. "I can run as fast as you."

Hare almost fell over laughing.

"I can," insisted Hedgehog, prickly.

"I'm built to run. Look at my legs, lean and powerful," replied Hare. "Do you even have legs under those spines?"

"Of course I do," replied Hedgehog. "I bet I can outrun you any time."

Hare snorted with laughter. "I'd like to see you try."

"Then let's have a race," said Hedgehog.

"Come on, let's go," said Hare, hopping from one foot to the other.

Just then the first of the sun's rays started to peek through the leaves. Hedgehog yawned. "I need to get some sleep," said Hedgehog. "I'll meet you on the ploughed field at midnight and prove to you I don't live in the slow lane."

"I'll see you then," said Hare, who sped off to find a good place to make his bed for the day.

Hedgehog knew he'd never be able to outrun Hare, so as he snuggled in his nest he came up with a plan. I'll need a little help from a friend and I know exactly who to ask, he thought as he closed his eyes.

•

The next evening Hedgehog got up a little early and visited his friend, who had built her nest among the roots of one of the old oak trees.

As he reached the oak trees he saw a small black shiny nose poke out from the roots and sniff the cool evening air. The nose was soon followed a ball of sharp prickles which looked just like Hedgehog.

"Hello," said Hedgehog.

"Hello,' came the reply. "How lovely to see you."

"I'm hoping you'll help me prove to Hare I'm faster than he is," said Hedgehog. "He's challenged me to a race and I accepted."

"You accepted? Why would you do that? You'll never win."

"I have a plan," said Hedgehog. "I'm hoping you'll help me."

"Of course I will. I've heard Hare boast about his speed. He needs to be taught a lesson."

So Hedgehog told his friend his plan and together they agreed to show Hare how fast a hedgehog could be.

•

Just before the church clock struck twelve Hedgehog and his friend arrived at the ploughed field. Hedgehog stood at the top of the field whilst his friend stood at the bottom. As the clock chimed twelve Hare bounded over to Hedgehog and skidded to a halt, spraying Hedgehog with small lumps of mud.

"Be careful," said Hedgehog, brushing the mud off his spines.

"Sorry," replied Hare with a large grin. "Are you ready to be beaten?"

Hedgehog smiled and ignored Hare's question. "To make it a fair race, I thought I could run along this furrow and you could run in that one," said Hedgehog, pointing. "The first to the bottom of the field is the winner."

Hare hopped over to the furrow Hedgehog had pointed at and patted the earth down with his large flat feet. "Ready when you are," said Hare, crouching down.

"On my count," said Hedgehog. "Three ... two ... one ... GO!"

Hare sped off, leaving a cloud of dust behind him, whilst Hedgehog took a few steps forward, turned around and lay down in the furrow. As he waited, Hedgehog smiled. He soon heard his friend's voice from the bottom of the field and his smile grew broader.

"Oh, you're here at last, Hare. I thought you'd got lost."

All Hare could see was a round prickly shape.

"How can that be? That's impossible!" shouted Hare.

"I'm happy to run the race again if you want," Hedgehog heard his friend reply.

"On my count," said Hare. "Three ... two ... one ... GO!"

Hare sped off, leaving a cloud of dust behind him, whilst Hedgehog's friend took a few steps forward, turned around and lay down in the furrow.

Hedgehog, lying in the furrow, could soon feel the pounding of Hare's feet on the ground. Just before Hare reached the point where Hedgehog was hiding Hedgehog got up and raced to the end of the furrow. He turned around and shouted, "Hare, at last! I'd given up on you."

"How can that be? That's impossible!" Hare gasped between breaths.

"I'm happy to run the race again if you want," said Hedgehog.

"Let's make it the best of five," puffed Hare.

"That's fine by me," replied Hedgehog. "On my count. Three ... two ... one ... GO!"

Again, Hare sped off, leaving a cloud of dust behind him whilst Hedgehog took a few steps and hid in the furrow. As the thud of Hare's feet became softer and softer, Hedgehog's smile became broader.

Soon Hedgehog heard his friend's voice drift up from the bottom of the field: "I'd almost given up waiting."

Hedgehog heard Hare shout between gasps, "Three ... two ... one ... GO!"

Again, Hedgehog lay in the furrow and could soon feel

the pounding of Hare's feet. Just before Hare reached where Hedgehog was hiding Hedgehog got up and raced to the end of the furrow. He turned around and shouted, "Do you give up?"

Hare collapsed beside Hedgehog and nodded. Finally, Hare found enough breath to wheeze, "I don't … know how y … you did it, but I … give up."

"Do I live in the slow lane?" asked Hedgehog.

Hare shook his head. "No, you don't," replied Hare.

● ● ●

"In times of trouble use your brains."

William Ellery Leonard (1876 – 1944)

HEDGEHOG HELPS MOTHER NATURE

One damp spring evening as he wandered along the lane, Hedgehog saw Mother Nature sitting on the top of the hill staring up at the sky.

"Good evening," he shouted. Mother Nature looked over her shoulder and gave Hedgehog a small smile. Feeling there was something wrong, Hedgehog decided to climb to the top of the hill.

Hedgehog sat beside Mother Nature and asked, "What are you looking at?"

"The stars and moon," she replied. "I should be happy when I look at them, but I'm not."

"Why?" asked Hedgehog. "They're beautiful."

"I know," replied Mother Nature. "But when I look at them I regret making the earth flat. I should've made it round, like the stars and the moon."

"Why don't you?" asked Hedgehog. "If you can't change it, who can?"

Mother Nature looked at Hedgehog and smiled. "You're right. It's not too late. But I'll need to take some measurements to make sure the earth still fits under the sky once I've made it round."

Mother Nature put her hand into a pocket and pulled out a large ball of string. "Can you hold this?" she asked Hedgehog, holding out the ball of string in one hand and taking the end of the string in the other.

Hedgehog smiled, held out his paw and took the ball of string.

"When the string becomes tight, just let it out a little," she said.

As Hedgehog watched Mother Nature take her measurements his stomach gave a long, low grumble. He looked around and noticed a large rotten log lying in the long grass. "There's bound to be something lovely to snack on under there," he thought. Hedgehog walked over to the log, put down the ball of string and lifted the log up. "Oh, these will be just right," he said to himself, popping a tasty morsel or two into his mouth. "Delicious."

Hedgehog suddenly realised the string had unravelled. "Whoops," he said, as he picked it up and began to wind it back up. Just as Hedgehog finished winding the ball of string back up Mother Nature appeared by his side.

"All done," she said, with a large smile on her face. "Now I have my measurements I can get to work."

"Great," said Hedgehog, handing back the ball of string.

"While you sleep, I'll make the earth round and tomorrow we can sit at the top of the hill and look up at the round stars and moon from a round earth."

"I look forward to it," said Hedgehog.

•

The next night Hedgehog found Mother Nature sitting on the top of the hill holding her face in her hands.

"What's the matter?" he asked.

"Haven't you noticed?"

"Noticed what?"

"There aren't any stars or moon."

Hedgehog looked up. He hadn't noticed. He'd been too busy looking for something to eat.

"I must've got my measurements wrong. I've made the earth too big and it won't fit under the sky anymore," Mother Nature said.

Hedgehog looked down at his feet for a moment as he remembered putting the string down.

"I've never made a mistake that big before," said Mother Nature. "I sometimes make little mistakes, but they always turn out all right in the end."

Hedgehog was sure he could see tears in her eyes and began to feel very guilty. I should've concentrated on holding the string and not looking for something to eat, he thought.

"I've no idea what to do," said Mother Nature. "I can't leave it like this. I'll have to make the earth flat again."

Hedgehog thought for a moment, then he had an inkling of an idea. "There's something you could try," he said.

"What?" asked Mother Nature.

"I'm not sure if it'll work, but you could try squeezing it smaller," he suggested.

Mother Nature thought for a while. "You know it may just work," she said.

•

The following day, as Hedgehog slept, Mother Nature took the earth carefully in her hands and gently squeezed. Slowly, she could feel the earth becoming smaller. As the earth became smaller, hills became bigger and steeper; some even became mountains capped with snow. As the earth became smaller valleys began to appear between the mountains. As the earth became smaller streams became rivers and rivers became seas. When the earth was small enough to fit under the sky again Mother Nature carefully put it back.

As the sun set over the new round earth Hedgehog poked his nose out of his nest and sniffed the air. He could sense something was different, but couldn't quite work out what it was. He crept out of his nest and made his way along the lane. There were small things that were different. The stream that followed the lane seemed deeper. When he looked at the hill he was sure it was steeper and the top was a little further away.

When he reached the path that led to the top of the hill Hedgehog noticed Mother Nature sitting, looking up at a sky filled with bright sparkling stars and a full moon. Hedgehog climbed the hill and as he reached Mother Nature she looked over her shoulder and gave a broad smile.

"Thank you, Hedgehog. Your idea worked," she said.

Hedgehog breathed a sigh of relief. Now he didn't have to own up to his little mistake.

• • •

"A hedgehog will bristle if you touch him."

German saying

HEDGEHOG AND STAG

No one knows how it came about, but Hedgehog and Stag owned a field together. One day, much to Hedgehog's surprise, Stag suggested they grow wheat in their field.

"I don't eat wheat," replied Hedgehog.

"Then what can we grow?" asked Stag.

Thinking for a moment, Hedgehog replied, "We could grow lettuce."

"But you don't eat lettuce either," said Stag, a little confused.

"No, but I can eat the insects that will feast on them all summer," said Hedgehog. "Then you can have all the lettuce in winter, when food becomes hard to find. That way we both gain."

"Good idea," said Stag.

And so it was agreed that Stag and Hedgehog would grow lettuce in their field.

•

All was going well until the lettuces began to grow thick and strong. Suddenly every creature of the woods was interested in the field and kept sneaking onto it to feast on the lettuce.

One morning when Hedgehog and Stag visited the field Hedgehog moaned, "We'll have nothing left at this rate. We'll have to start guarding it."

"I'm happy to guard it during the day," said Stag.

"Then I'll guard it at night," said Hedgehog.

The plan went well for the first few days and nights, until one evening, when Hedgehog turned up for guard duty and found many of the lettuces missing and Stag asleep in the middle of the field.

Hedgehog stomped over to Stag, his prickles raised, and woke him up.

"What happened to our crop?" Hedgehog asked Stag.

"Some of my herd came to see me and we ate a few," said Stag. "They just looked too good."

"That's not fair. That means I'll have fewer insects to eat during the summer," said Hedgehog.

Stag looked apologetic. "I'm sorry. It won't happen again."

Stag joined his herd whilst Hedgehog ensured the remaining lettuces were safe from the insects that wanted to feast on them.

Just before sunrise Stag returned and Hedgehog went off to sleep the day away.

The next night, when Hedgehog returned, he found even more of the lettuces had been eaten.

"This can't keep happening," said Hedgehog. "I'm holding up my end of the deal."

"It won't," said Stag, but it did.

•

Finally, it came time to harvest the lettuces that remained.

"I'm going to harvest what's left," said Hedgehog, "and I'm going to keep the lot."

"That's not fair," said Stag. "I made sure no one else ate any."

"But each time you ate some lettuces there was less for me to eat. The deal was I ate the insects and when the time came you could have all the lettuces," said Hedgehog.

Hedgehog and Stag just couldn't agree. They argued and argued until sunrise.

Just then Goat came by. He stopped and listened to Hedgehog and Stag arguing.

"I'll mediate," he said.

Hedgehog and Stag accepted Goat's offer and explained what had happened.

"It sounds very complicated," said Goat. "So I can make a fair decision, I'll have to go away and think about it. Meet me here at sunset and I'll tell you what I've decided."

Hedgehog and Stag agreed. Hedgehog then went to sleep the day away.

Whilst Hedgehog slept Goat and Stag met and came to an arrangement.

"If I give all the lettuces to you," said Goat, "you have to give me half."

"Agreed," said Stag. "What if Hedgehog argues?"

"I'll suggest a race and winner takes all," replied Goat.

"Great," said Stag. "There's no way Hedgehog can win a race against me."

•

The next evening Hedgehog, Stag and Goat met in the field.

"I think Stag should get every lettuce," Goat said. "That was the original agreement."

"But each time Stag and his herd ate the lettuces I had fewer insects to catch," said Hedgehog. "So I deserve some of the lettuces as compensation."

"But I kept everyone in the forest away from the lettuces," said Stag.

"Apart from your herd," said Hedgehog, "who ate more than their fill."

"The only way I can see of settling this argument is to have a race," said Goat. "The winner takes all."

Hedgehog smiled and thought, Stag thinks he'll win, but I have a small trick I can play.

"I'm happy with that," said Stag.

"Me too," said Hedgehog.

Stag and Hedgehog took their places at the top of the field.

"Are you ready?" asked Goat.

Hedgehog and Stag nodded.

As Stag crouched down and got ready to run Hedgehog got ready to jump.

"Three … two … one … GO!" shouted Goat.

Just as Stag sped off along the field, Hedgehog leapt up and grabbed Stag's antlers. Closing his eyes, Hedgehog concentrated on holding on as tightly as he could.

Stag looked over his shoulder. He couldn't see

Hedgehog anywhere. "This'll be a breeze," he said, as he raced along the furrows towards the bottom of the field.

Stag looked over his shoulder again. He still couldn't see Hedgehog. "Keep going," he said to himself. "Almost there."

Hedgehog opened his eyes. "Any time now," he said.

I'm winning by a mile, thought Stag, looking over his shoulder again.

Hedgehog got ready to let go.

Almost there, thought Stag.

As Hedgehog let go, he pushed himself forward over Stag's head. He flew through the air and landed with a soft thump just on the finish line. He rolled and came to a stop near the stone wall. Quickly uncurling, he looked up to see Stag just crossing the line.

"That can't be!" shouted Stag.

"We made a deal," said Hedgehog.

"I know," said Stag, grudgingly.

Hedgehog watched and smiled as Stag and Goat left the field arguing.

Hedgehog licked his lips and began to feast. As he did he thought, I'll leave the lettuces for anyone who wants them.

• • •

"The best way to get rid of intruders is never to let them in."

William Bentley Fowle (1795 – 1865)

HEDGHOG AND THE BILLY GOAT

Hedgehog had just got up from his slumber when there was an enormous flash of lightning. Hedgehog began slowly to count: "one, two, three, four, five, six, seven." He stopped counting for a moment, expecting the thunder to arrive. It didn't.

"Good, I have time before the storm arrives," he said, just as the expected thunder rumbled across the sky.

Hedgehog thought for a moment and decided to make his way along the lane. As he trotted along he heard the familiar voice of Fox. "Get OUT, GET OUT, I say."

Hedgehog stopped for a moment, then his stomach grumbled. "I'm sure Fox doesn't need my help. He's does have seventy-seven wits after all." So Hedgehog continued his walk along the lane.

A little later Hedgehog overheard Hare and Rabbit chatting.

"Have you heard, Fox can't get into his den," said Hare.

"Why not?" asked Rabbit.

"There's a billy goat standing in the doorway," replied Hare.

"It must be a large billy goat, otherwise Fox would easily shoo it out," said Rabbit.

Hedgehog smiled as he thought, That billy goat doesn't stand a chance against Fox.

While Hedgehog was looking for something to eat among the leaves under the oak trees he overheard Little Owl and Big Owl talking.

"Have you heard, Fox can't get into his den," said Little Owl.

"Why not?" asked Big Owl.

"There's a billy goat standing in the doorway," replied Little Owl. "I've also heard Fox had to ask Badger for help."

"It must be a big billy goat," said Big Owl.

"It is," replied Little Owl. "I've heard even Badger hasn't managed to get it to move."

Hedgehog was surprised by what he heard, but was far too busy to go and offer help.

Some time later, when Hedgehog was tucking into a bowl of cat food the farmer's wife had left out for him, he heard a scurry of small feet. He looked around and saw Mouse coming out of hiding and picking up a juicy blackberry that had fallen off a bush.

Hedgehog stopped eating for a moment. "Good evening, Mouse. How are you?"

"Fine, thank you," she replied. Then she said, "Have you heard, Fox and Badger can't get a billy goat out of Fox's den. They've even had to ask Stag for help."

"Really?" asked Hedgehog. "How big is this billy goat?"

"I've heard it's a monster," replied Mouse.

"I think I'll go home via Fox's den and offer some help," Hedgehog said.

Mouse's eye became wide. "You're braver than I am," she said, just before she disappeared under the bush, still clutching her blackberry.

As Hedgehog licked the plate clean he thought, This billy goat must be the monster everyone is saying it is. Otherwise Fox, Badger and Stag would be able to get it to leave Fox's den.

Once Hedgehog was sure the plate was clean he made his way to Fox's den. When he got there, he was surprised to see Fox, Badger and Stag standing some way back from Fox's den. Hedgehog walked over to them and asked Fox, "Why is there a billy goat in your den?"

Fox pointed to the field. "It was scared by the thunder, jumped over the fence and bolted into my den," he told Hedgehog.

"He can't be that fierce if he is scared of a little thunder," said Hedgehog.

A small "meh-meh" came from Fox's den.

Fox, Badger and Stag took a small step back.

"He doesn't sound that big," said Hedgehog.

"His horns are longer and stronger than my antlers," said Stag. "I'm not trying to get it out."

Another small "meh-meh" came from Fox's den.

Fox, Badger and Stag took another small step back.

"Are you sure none of you can get him out?" asked Hedgehog.

"His hooves are stronger and sharper than my claws," said Badger. "I'm not trying to get it out."

Another small "meh-meh" came from Fox's den.

Fox, Badger and Stag took yet another small step back.

"Just how big is this billy goat?" asked Hedgehog.

"He can turn and bite you quicker than I can," said Fox. "I'm not trying to get it out."

Another small "meh-meh" came from Fox's den.

Fox, Badger and Stag took yet another small step back.

"He really doesn't sound that big," said Hedgehog. "Do you want me to see if I can get him out?"

Fox, Badger and Stag laughed.

"Give it a go," said Fox, smirking.

"Yes, I'd like to see you try," said Badger.

"You'd better open the gate," said Hedgehog, annoyed and with his spines raised slightly. "This billy goat is coming out!"

There was another small "meh-meh" from Fox's den. Fox, Stag and Badger looked at one another and made a dash to open the gate.

Fox, Stag and Badger stood behind the gate for protection as Hedgehog stomped across the grass and into Fox's den.

When he got inside Hedgehog looked around expecting to see a fierce billy goat with long horns, strong claws and sharp teeth. But all he saw was a small white billy goat, shivering with fright in the corner.

"Meh, meh," it bleated again.

Hedgehog knew exactly what to do. He climbed up the

wall and sat on a small ledge. He rolled himself into a tight ball and pushed himself off the ledge towards the small white billy goat.

"Meh, meh," it bleated. "Meh … MEH!" Hedgehog hit its rump with a thump. "MEH, MEH!" it bleated. Hedgehog unrolled himself and watched the small billy goat dash out of Fox's den. As he got to the entrance he saw an anxious-looking mother goat greet her baby with a soothing bleat while Fox, Badger and Stag quickly closed the gate behind it.

• • •

"One knavery of the hedgehog is worth more than the many of the fox."

Arabic proverb

CLEVER HEDGEHOG

One late autumn evening Hedgehog decided to see if he could find something nice to eat in the orchard. Sometimes there were insects busying themselves feeding on the fallen fruit and the last of the flowers before winter arrived. As he foraged he heard the familiar voices of Fox and Badger. Typically, they were boasting and trying to outdo one another. Hedgehog smiled and thought, Perhaps I could outdo them. So Hedgehog went over to where the two were sitting.

"Oh hello," said Hedgehog, pretending to be surprised. "I didn't see you there. How are you both?"

"Well," replied Fox.

"I'm even better," boasted Badger, unable to stop himself.

Just then a single large juicy damson fell to the ground, landing with a soft thump on the grass.

"A pity that's not big enough to share," said Hedgehog.

"Yes, a pity," said Badger.

"A great pity," agreed Fox.

Hedgehog had an idea. "Why don't we have a

competition? The winner wins the damson," he suggested.

"A good idea," said Fox.

"A brilliant idea," agreed Badger. "But what?"

Hedgehog thought. "Perhaps …" He pondered briefly, then smiled. "We can all do things that are hard, but how about sharing something we find easy to do? Whoever can do something the easiest wins the damson."

"But what?" asked Badger.

As Hedgehog racked his brains Fox said, "I can get drunk easily."

"You can?" asked Badger.

"Oh yes," said Fox. "I remember the time when I was outside the farmer's barn when he was bottling cider. A few of the bottles exploded and it covered the cobbles in the yard."

"I remember that," said Badger.

"Well," said Fox, giving Badger a sideways glance. "I got so drunk on the cider I decided I'd never drink it again."

As Badger and Hedgehog listened Hedgehog started to wobble slightly from side to side.

"For the rest of the day and the next I had a thumping headache." Fox continued.

"I remember that day well. I became drunk from just breathing in the cider fumes," said Badger. "I'm never going near cider again. I had a thumping headache for the rest of the day and for the next two days."

Fox noticed Hedgehog was wobbling.

"Hedgehog, are you all right?" asked Fox.

"I think I'm fine," Hedgehog said. "I just feel a little

light-headed. Keep going. I love listening to your stories."

Not wanting to be outdone by his friend, Fox boasted, "I find it so easy that just eating a couple of ripened cider apples makes me drunk."

As Fox continued to brag about how easy it was for him to get drunk Hedgehog wobbled over to the base of the damson tree and sat down.

"Are you all right?" Badger asked Hedgehog. "You look a little odd."

Hedgehog waved a paw and gave a lopsided smile. "I'm fine," he said. "Please carry on."

Not wanting to be outdone by his friend, Badger boasted, "I find it so easy I only have to eat half a ripened cider apple and I'm drunk."

As Hedgehog listened to his friends boasting he started to slide down the tree and was soon slumped to one side with a large grin on his face.

"Are you all right?" asked Badger.

"Yes, you look decidedly unwell," said Fox.

"Jusht a lit' giddy," said Hedgehog.

Not wanting to be outdone by his friend, Fox continued to boast. "I find it so easy to get drunk that if I go into the orchard and smell the ripened cider apples I'm drunk."

As Hedgehog listened to his two friends boasting he gave a couple of soft hiccups.

Badger ignored the hiccupping hedgehog and boasted, "I only have to stand at the edge of the orchard when the ripened cider apples are being harvested and I'm drunk."

A large hiccup erupted from Hedgehog. "Shorrie," he

said, with a little giggle.

"Are you all right, Hedgehog?" asked Fox.

"You don't look or sound yourself at all," said Badger.

"Jusht a – " Hiccup. "A lil' … a lil' bit –" Hiccup.

"Hedgehog, are you drunk?" asked Fox.

"He can't be drunk!" said Badger.

"I'm shorrie," said Hedgehog, as he rocked to and fro on his back. "Jusht listhening to you hash made m' thunk."

Badger looked at Fox and Fox looked at Badger.

"I think Hedgehog has won the damson fruit," they said in unison.

"Hreally?" asked Hedgehog.

"Oh, yes," said Fox.

"Most definitely," added Badger.

Hedgehog rolled on to his front and managed to stand up. "I'll eat this on my way home," he said. "What way is home?"

Badger and Fox pointed.

Hedgehog let out a couple of huge hiccups, turned around slowly and pretended to stagger across the meadow. As he left he heard the soft thud of another damson fruit as it hit the long grass.

"It's pity that's too small to share," said Badger.

"Do you know what I find easy?" asked Fox.

"What?" asked Badger.

• • •

CLEVER HEDGEHOG

"A kindness in never wasted."

Aesop (620BC – 560BC)

HEDGEHOG AND THE ANTS

One very warm evening Hedgehog woke earlier than normal. As he stretched and yawned he thought, I need a drink. He peeked out of his nest and the evening light blinded him for a moment. "Bother that sun," he said.

Hedgehog sniffed the air. Good, it's all clear, he thought as he slowly crept out into the evening sunlight. He checked for danger again, then headed towards the hedge. Keeping to the shadows, he scurried in the direction of the small brook. As he wove in and out of the tall grasses, they rustled in time with his movements. Every so often he stopped to root around in the long grass and look for something to eat. Much to his delight he found an array of insects, including a very large, juicy green caterpillar and a black, crunchy bug. As he munched on an extremely long millipede he pondered. I wonder, he thought, if there'll be the usual plate of food under the wheelbarrow. Hopefully that cat won't have beaten me to it.

Hedgehog eventually reached the gate that led into the bottom field. He looked around: the coast was clear. So, he dashed from one side of the gate to the other. When he reached the other side, he paused and checked again. This time in the distance he could see several silhouettes slowly moving in the field. He sniffed the air but the breeze was blowing in the wrong direction. "I'm sure they're far enough away not to be a bother," he told himself.

Hedgehog continued to weave his way along the hedge, looking for tasty morsels as he went. When he reached the corner of the bottom field, Hedgehog squeezed through the gap in the hedge to get to the track the other side. He stopped, sniffed the air and listened. All he could hear was the soft rustle of the leaves in the trees. Feeling safe, he scurried across the track and squeezed himself in among the long grasses and nettles. Almost there, he thought as he made his way down a shallow bank.

When he reached the bottom of the bank Hedgehog smiled. "How lovely," he said, watching the light filter through the trees and play on the surface of the brook. "Reminds me of the time when Mother Nature and I sat on the hill looking up at the stars."

Hedgehog scurried down to the edge of the brook and tentatively dipped a toe in. "Oh, lovely and cool," he said, as he waded a little further in and started to paddle along the brook. Every so often he stopped and took a drink of the crisp, clean water. "What a wonderful evening," he said. After a while Hedgehog remembered the bowl of food in the farmer's garden. "I think it's time to discover what's on that plate," he said, as he waded out of the water and onto the bank.

As he shook his feet dry Hedgehog noticed a small path

leading down from the bottom field to the brook. I wonder who uses that? he thought. Perhaps I can use it as a short cut to the garden.

As he turned to walk up the small path he saw movement out of the corner of his eye. He stopped and stared. He then noticed a large yellowing leaf caught on a rock in the water. "How did you get stuck there?" he asked, watching a small army of ants running around the leaf, desperately trying to find a way off. Hedgehog watched them for a moment or two then made a decision. My first good deed for tonight, he thought, looking around for something to help the ants escape. Seeing a stick gently bobbing up and down at the edge of the water, he scurried over to it and picked it up. He then carefully balanced one end on the rock and the other end on the bank.

The ants didn't move. Hedgehog smiled. "Go ahead. I won't eat you," he told them. The first ant crept off the leaf, onto the rock and then onto the stick. The stick wobbled a little as the ant ran along it. Once he reached the bank the ant turned and signalled to the other ants. When they saw that it was safe they ran in single file from the leaf to the rock and along the stick. Hedgehog watched as they marched in single file up the bank and into a crack under a large weather-worn rock.

Just as the last ant disappeared into their nest Hedgehog heard a noise behind him. He froze. He heard the crunch of a footstep on the pebbled bank. Hedgehog instantly pulled himself into a tight ball. He waited and waited, but apart from the soft bubbling of the brook there was no other sound. So he slowly relaxed and uncurled. As he uncurled he became aware of someone softly and slowly breathing. It could be Fox playing a trick on me. It wouldn't be the first time, he thought. Hedgehog didn't move, nor did whoever was standing near him. Nervously, he uncurled enough to take a peek. They're not Fox's paws, he thought.

"It is you," he heard someone say.

"Who's that?" Hedgehog asked.

"You scared my baby," came the reply.

Hedgehog thought for a moment, then he worked out who it was. He swallowed hard, uncurled and looked up into the scowling face of Nanny Goat.

"He wouldn't come out of Fox's den," said Hedgehog. "I was only trying to help."

"He was scared," Nanny Goat replied.

"Fox tried to entice him out with some lovely grass," said Hedgehog, beginning to feel more than a little nervous. "Honestly, everyone tried to coax him out very gently but everyone was just bitten and butted in return."

"That's not the story he told me," said Nanny Goat, taking a step forward.

"We ..." said Hedgehog.

"There was no need to roll into him with your prickles up," said Nanny Goat. "I was pulling them out of my baby for days. You're all big bullies."

"I ..." replied Hedgehog, but Nanny Goat didn't give him a chance to finish.

"You could've found another way," she said as she

lowered her head. Hedgehog could smell her grassy breath as it ruffled his spines.

"We tried everything we could think of," replied Hedgehog.

"You didn't try hard enough," Nanny Goat replied. "Why didn't you come and find me?"

"We ..."

"Now you're going to find out what it's like to be butted by an angry mother goat."

"Please ..."

"No! You scared my baby," said Nanny Goat.

Then out of the corner of his eye Hedgehog saw a line of ants hurrying down the bank towards him. He stepped back a little and found himself standing in the water again. Just as Nanny Goat lowered her head to line her horns up with Hedgehog the first ant reached her. Hedgehog stepped back a little further and watched as the ants climbed up one of Nanny Goat's legs.

"What ..." she bleated, as the ants nipped at her fur and flesh. They nipped and nipped. "Get off! Get off!" Nanny Goat bleated as she kicked her back legs out, trying to shake the ants off.

"Thank you, friends," said Hedgehog, quickly making his escape.

When he reached the top of the small path Hedgehog thought, now where was I? Oh, yes that bowl of food under the wheelbarrow.

• • •

"There goes the swallow, could we but follow!
Hasty swallow, stay, point us out the way;
Look back swallow, turn back swallow, stop swallow."

Christina G. Rossetti (1830 – 1894)

HEDGEHOG AND THE YOUNG SWALLOW

Hedgehog was rooting around in a pile of old straw heaped in the corner of the barnyard when he heard a swoosh above his head. He quickly curled up and waited for a moment. Silly me, I should be used to that sound by now, he thought as he slowly uncurled. Once uncurled, he looked up into the pale blue sky. He smiled as he watched one of the swallow fledglings darting back and forth across the yard practising its flying skills. The cobalt blue on its head, the rusty-red of its chin and the thin white line on its forked tail glistened in the fading rays of sunlight. As he watched, a movement by his feet caught his eye. A couple of bugs he'd disturbed were making a dash for safety. Hedgehog pounced and quickly added them to the day's bug count.

"Why are you always eating?" asked a small voice.

Hedgehog jumped and choked on the shiny black, very crunchy bug he'd just swallowed.

"Sorry," said the voice. "I didn't mean to make you jump."

Hedgehog looked up and perched on the guttering of

the cowshed was the swallow fledgling.

Hedgehog smiled. "Don't worry," he said. "I'm more than used to it. My old friend Fox does it to me all the time."

"Why are you always eating?" asked the young swallow again. "I never see you do anything else."

Hedgehog loved the bluntness of the very young. They had no filters on the questions they asked, which meant you always knew where you stood with them.

"Winter's on its way and I have to put on weight so I can hibernate," he told her.

"What's winter?" asked the young swallow.

"Do you remember last week when we had that horrendous storm with the thunder, lightning and whipping cold wind?" asked Hedgehog.

"It was awful. I've never been that cold before," said the young swallow. "I was sure our nest was going to be washed away."

"Imagine that day after day," said Hedgehog. "That's what we call winter."

"So, what's 'hibernate' mean?" asked the young swallow.

Hedgehog thought for a moment. "Well, it's not sleeping, but it is," he said. "I build myself a nest and sleep the winter away."

"What a good idea," said the young swallow.

"That's why I'm always eating. I have to eat all the meals I'll miss when I hibernate," he said.

"All of them?" she asked, in disbelief.

Hedgehog's eyes twinkled. "My grandma used to tell me

swallows hibernate as well. But you make your nest in the mud at the edge of the pond."

"Really?" asked the young swallow. "Mama has never told me this."

"That's what my grandma told me," he replied.

"Oh my," said the young swallow. "I'd better get ready for winter. I'm off to the pond to catch enough flies for three meals."

Hedgehog watched the young swallow as she darted across the sky. "I'm obviously spending too much time with Fox," he said. "That's the type of trick he'd play."

•

The next evening Hedgehog was squeezing under the garden gate when he heard the familiar swoosh, swoosh of the young swallows overhead. Once inside the garden he stopped for a moment and looked up into the pale blue sky. He smiled as he watched the three swallow fledglings practising their flying. Keep practising, little ones, you'll need those skills, he thought. He then headed towards the upturned wheelbarrow, where he hoped a bowl of food had been left for him.

Scurrying across the short grass, he heard the swoosh, swoosh again and just as he reached the flower bed he heard a familiar voice.

"Hello, Hedgehog."

Looking up, he saw the silhouette of the young swallow who was perched on the thin, swaying yellow washing line.

"Hello," replied Hedgehog, hoping the swallow fledging wouldn't hold him up for too long.

"I did as you suggested," she said.

"You did?" he asked.

"Yes, I tried to eat three meals at once. But I felt so, so sick afterwards. I don't know how you do it."

"I'm sorry to hear that," said Hedgehog, feeling a little guilty for playing the trick on the swallow fledging.

"What should I do?" she asked.

Hedgehog's guilt quickly faded and he smiled. "Well, you could do what Squirrel does," he said. "She doesn't eat all her meals at once, but collects nuts and stores them for when she's hungry."

"That's a good idea. Thank you," said the young swallow as she spread her graceful wings and took off.

•

A little later Hedgehog saw the young swallow with a full beak of insects carefully placing them in an old, abandoned nest under the eaves of the farmhouse.

"That looks like a good catch," he shouted to her.

"It was," she called back. "It's hard work catching three meals."

Hedgehog smiled and thought, now I can see why Fox plays his tricks. I know it's naughty, but it is fun.

•

Again, and again the young swallow returned to the nest and carefully filled it with the extra insects she'd caught.

As she placed her last catch of the day in the old nest she heard a delicate flap of wings. She turned her head and saw her mother sitting on the guttering of the old farmhouse.

"Hello, Mama," said the young swallow, joining her

mama.

"What are you doing, darling?" asked Mama Swallow.

"Hedgehog told me we hibernate in the mud of the pond," replied the swallow fledging. "So, I'm getting ready."

"He did, did he?" replied Mama Swallow, looking amused.

"Yesterday I tried to eat three meals to make up for some I'd miss when we hibernate, but it made me feel very unwell," the fledging told her mama.

"That explains why you wiggled and kept us all awake last night," said Mama Swallow, with a small sigh.

"So I'm doing what Squirrel does," said the young swallow.

Mama Swallow smiled. "I think Hedgehog's spending too much time with his friend Fox," she said. "He's playing a trick on you, darling. We don't hibernate; we go on an adventure to somewhere new."

"Where do we go?" asked the young swallow.

"We go to the other side of the world," replied Mama Swallow.

"How will I know how to get there?" asked the young swallow, becoming a little worried. "I might get lost."

"We go together," replied Mama Swallow. "It's a long and hard journey, but as we fly we'll see wonderful new and exciting things."

"What type of things?" asked the young swallow.

"You'll see a pond the size you could only dream of. We'll fly over hills that reach the sky. You'll see forests that go on forever and you'll make new friends," Mama Swallow told her.

"Who?" asked the young swallow.

"They'll be very different to your friends here," said Mama Swallow. "One will remind you of Horse, but this horse has black and white stripes."

"When can we go?" asked the young swallow, her feathers rustling in excitement.

"In a few days," replied Mama Swallow.

"So, I don't have to eat all my missed meals?"

"No, darling."

"And I don't have to store food?"

"No, darling," replied Mama Swallow. "Go and play with your brother and sister while I go and have a little chat with that naughty Hedgehog."

• • •

BONUS CONTENT

Whilst researching for this book I found some of the stories have been retold in many ways. As these versions are in the public domain, I've included them on the following pages.

I hope you enjoy.

HEDGEHOG, FOX AND FLIES
VERSION ONE

"Sick in a ditch, one sultry day,
Devoured by flies, poor Reynard lay,
And loud complained of fortune's spite,
That left him in such a grievous plight.
A Hedgehog, passing by that way
(His first appeared in my play),
Proposed, with neighbourly attention,
To rid him of the pests I mention.
The Fox a beast of prudent mind
At once, with many thanks, declined.
'I dread,' he said, 'with more alarm,
A fresh and therefore hungrier swarm.
These have well fed, and, though not pleasant,
Will bite less keenly for the present."

La Fontaine and Other French Fabulists
Rev. William Lucas Collins (1817-1887)

HEDGEHOG, FOX AND FLIES
VERSION TWO

A fox, old, subtle, vigilant, and sly,
By hunters wounded, fallen in the mud,
Attracted, by the traces of his blood,
That buzzing parasite, the fly.
He blamed the gods, and wonder'd why
The fates so cruelly should wish
To feast the fly on such a costly dish.
'What! Light on me! Make me its food!
Me, me, the nimblest of the wood!
How long has fox-meat been so good?
What serves my tail? Is it a useless weight?
Go, heaven confound thee, greedy reprobate,
And suck thy fill from some more vulgar veins!'
A hedgehog, witnessing his pains,
(This fretful personage
Here graces first my page)
Desired to set him free
From such cupidity.
'My neighbour fox,' said he,
My quills these rascals shall empale,

And ease thy torments without fail.'
'Not for the world, my friend!' the fox replied.
'Pray let them finish their repast.
These flies are full. Should they be set aside,
New hungrier swarms would finish me at last.'
Consumers are too common here below,
In court and camp, in church and state, we know.
Old Aristotle's penetration
Remark'd our fable's application;
It might more clearly in our nation.
The fuller certain men are fed,
The less the public will be bled.

The Fables of La Fontaine
Translated from the French by Elizur Wright (1804-1885)

HEDGEHOG, FOX AND FLIES
VERSION THREE

A Fox who swam across a torrent
Was swept along by wave and current
Into a dank and dark ravine,
Where long he lay, until gangrene
Set in and made him most unclean
And wretched. (For upon the rocks
He'd gotten scratches, bruises, knocks.)
Besides, the vile retreat was warm.
So soon there settled down a swarm
Of sucking flies upon the Fox.
The Hedgehog came commiserating,
In kindly words his purpose stating:
"I'll drive the horrid flies away."
"No, gentle Hedgehog, let them stay.
For these same flies are full of gore,
So full they can't suck any more.
They sting me little. I am freighted
At present with the satiated.
But should they leave, their hungry kin
Would come, and stick their suckers in,
And drink the blood that yet remains."

Moral:
In times of trouble use your brains.

Aesop and Hyssop; being fables adapted and original with the morals carefully formulated, William Ellery Leonard (1876-1944)

HEDGEHOG, FOX AND FLIES
VERSION FOUR

A Fox, upon the crossing of a river, was forc'd away by the current into the eddy, and there he lay with whole swarms of flies sucking and galling of him. There was a Water-Hedge-Hog (we must imagine) at hand, that in pure pity offer'd to beat away the flies for him. No, no, says the Fox, pray let 'em alone, for the flies that are upon me now are e'en bursting-full already, and can do me little more hurt than they have done: But when these are gone once, there will be a company you shall see of starv'd hungry wretches to take their places, that will not leave so much as one drop of blood in the whole body of me.

Fables of Aesop and Other Eminent Mythologists: With Morals and Reflections (8th edition), Sir Roger L'Estrange (1616-1704)

THE SNAKE AND THE HEDGEHOG
VERSION ONE

"Soon as he felt the winter frosts begin,
A Hedgehog begged a Snake to take him in:
'Twill be a deed of charity,' said he.
'I'm perishing with cold, as you may see;
    And then
In this great hole how lonely you will be,
All by yourself, till summer comes again!
    So take me under cover
I'm first-rate company, as you'll discover.'
    The Snake consented,
    And very soon repented.
The Hedgehog proved a most unpleasant guest;
    Curled himself up into a horrid ball,
    Rolled here and there, with no regard at all
For his poor hostess, who could get no rest,
    And even pricked her side
With those sharp-pointed quills upon his hide.
    Vainly she made complaint;
It was the brute's amusement so to do.
Such conduct would provoke a saint.

At last she said, 'Behave yourself, or go!'
'Go!' said the brute. 'Not I! I'm here at present,
    And here I'll stay:
Go out yourself, if you find things unpleasant!'
In a companion one may find a master.
    A solitary life is dull, you say;
Life with a Hedgehog is a worse disaster."

La Fontaine and Other French Fabulists,
William Lucas Collins (1817-1887)

THE SNAKE AND THE HEDGEHOG
VERSION TWO

A snake was prevail'd upon in a cold winter, to take a hedge-hog into his cell; but when he was once in, the place was so narrow, that the prickles of the hedge-hog were very troublesome to his companion: so that the snake told him, he must needs provide for himself somewhere else, for the hole was not big enough to hold them both. Why then, says the hedge-hog, he that cannot stay, shall do well to go: But for my own part, I'm e'en content where I am; and if you be not so too, y'are free to remove.

Moral:
Possession is Eleven Points of the Law

Fables of Aesop and Other Eminent Mythologists: With Morals and Reflections (8th edition), Sir Roger L'Estrange (1616-1704)

The above also appears with almost the same wording in: *Aesop's Fables: with instructive morals and reflections from all party considerations, adapted to all capacitates, and design'd to promote religion, morality and universal benevolence* ... and *The Life of*

Aesop, Richard Samuel (1689-1761) but with the moral:

It is not safe to join interests with strangers upon such terms as to lay ourselves at their mercy.

THE HEDGEHOG AND THE MOLE

The Hedgehog, when he found that the winter drew near, asked the Mole to spare him a little place in his hole, that he might be protected from the cold. The Mole agreed; but no sooner had the Hedgehog gained admittance, then he began to make himself comfortable, and to spread himself out, so that his host was pricked himself every moment, now here, now there, with the hard bristles of his new guest.

The poor Mole now perceived the consequences of his rashness; protested that this was quite intolerable to him, and in short desired the Hedgehog to depart, as his small dwelling could not possibly contain them both. But the Hedgehog laughed, and said, "Whoever is displeased with his situation, let him depart! I, for my part, am well contented, and shall remain."

Moral:
Reflect first, whom thou wilt take into thy intimate companionship; if he prove an unsociable person, thou mayst then be obliged to make room to thine own damage.

Fables and Parable from the German of Lessing, Herder (Krummacher and others), James Burns (1808-1871)

Dear Reader

Thank you for buying and reading this book.

We hope you enjoyed this collection of Moon Meadow Farm stories. If you have, would you mind leaving a quick review on Amazon? As an indie publisher reviews help readers find us and our books.

Thank you from the Mad Moment Media team.

To find out about our other books please visit us at:
www.madmomentmedia.com

BIBLIOGRAPHY

Information and websites to the original versions of the bonus stories included in this book.

Hedgehog, Fox and Flies – Version One (page 9 in the book below)
The Snake and the Hedgehog – Version One (page 143 in the book below)
La Fontaine and Other French Fabulists, Rev. William Lucas Collins (1817-1887)
Published by W. Blackwood (1882)
To view this book search: archive.org

Hedgehog, Fox and Flies – Version Two (Book XII, Story 24 in the book below)
The Fables of La Fontaine translated from the French by Elizur Wright (1804-1885)
Published by J W M Gibbs (1882)
To view this book search: www.gutenberg.org

Hedgehog, Fox and Flies – Version Three (page 99 in the book below)

Aesop and Hyssop; being fables adapted and original with the morals carefully formulated, William Ellery Leonard (1876-1944)
Published by Open Court Publishing Co, Chicago (1912)
To view this book search: www.hathitrust.org

Hedgehog, Fox and Flies – Version Four (page 268, Fable 254 in the book below)
The Snake and the Hedgehog – Version Two (page 336, Fable 324 in the book below)
Fables of Aesop and Other Eminent Mythologists: With Morals and Reflections (8th edition), Sir Roger L'Estrange (1616-1704)
Published by A. Bettesworth et al (1738)
To view this book search: https://books.google.co.uk

The Hedgehog and the Mole (page 46, Fable 73 in the book below)
Fables and Parables from the German of Lessing, Herder (Krummacher and others), James Burns (1808-1871)
Published by WM. Davy and Son (1845)
To view this book search: https://books.google.co.uk

Morals

"The best way to get rid of intruders is never to let them in."
Fowles French Fables, William Bentley Fowle (1795-1865), Sanborn, Carter and Bazin, Portland (1856)

"It is not safe to join interests with strangers upon such terms as to lay ourselves at their mercy." (page 250, Fable 192)

Aesop's Fables: with instructive morals and reflections from all party considerations, adapted to all capacitates, and design'd to promote religion, morality and universal benevolence ... and *The Life of Aesop*, Richard Samuel (1689-1761). J. Osborn junior (1740) To view this book search: archive.org

ABOUT THE AUTHOR

Lynne started writing professionally in 1997; mainly for UK-based magazines. Since that time, she has had over 25 books and more than 300 features published. Her books have been published in UK, USA, Canada, Holland, Australia, Korea and Indonesia. Her first picture book, *A Book For Bramble*, has been translated into five languages, whilst her second book, *The Best Jumper*, was recorded and aired on the BBC's CBeeBies radio channel.

To learn more about Lynne and her work visit:
www.lynnegarner.com

To find out more about Hedgehog and his friends, and to keep up to date with all their news please like the author's Facebook page.

www.facebook.com/lynnegarnerauthor

OTHER BOOKS AVAILABLE NOW

Anansi The Trickster Spider
Ten Tales of Brer Rabbit
Ten Tales of Coyote

BOOKS COMING SOON

Fox of Moon Meadow Farm

www.facebook.com/madmomentmedia
www.madmomentmedia.com

Made in the USA
Columbia, SC
22 March 2018